FLESH & BLOOD

Flesh & Blood

(Blood Rights, Book Nine)

K. B. Thorne

This book is dedicated to communities—those we enter, those we find, those we create, those we nurture—whether they are in-person or online, blood or found family.

Chapter One

I t was a showdown.

A contest of wills.

I stared at him. He stared at me.

Neither of us blinked.

Really, we didn't. Vampires don't need to blink.

He broke first.

"I won't do it!" he exclaimed, and not for the first time.

"Oh, come on!" I all but pleaded.

Vance was sitting in the armchair beside the couch, of which I occupied one end while Madison took up the other. We had our knees up and notepads out with pens at the ready, working on ideas and plans for the Fourth of July celebration that the town would be hosting. I had spent the past fifteen minutes trying to talk Vance into him and some of the other cops being the victims of the dunking booth to raise money. He was stalwartly refusing me.

Gabriel walked out of the kitchen with two wine glasses filled with rich red liquid, but in this case, it was just Merlot for him and Madison. She flashed him a smile, and the gold band on her left hand flashed as she took the glass from him.

The silver band on her right hand joined it.

It wasn't the life I would've pictured for her, but she seemed exceedingly happy with her special situation. Even months out, it still radiated from her.

"Sadie," she said, turning to me and pulling my attention from my... Well, it wasn't introspection because it wasn't about me. Outrospection? Was that a thing? She went on, "Why are we even doing this? Aren't there people who, you know, work for the city that should be doing this?"

"I volunteered," I said with a shrug, picking up my own wine glass—Type B-positive, 2016, a very good year—and took a sip.

"You are a glutton for punishment," she said with a smirk.

I went on. "It's not like the town suffers an abundance of people with nothing else to do, and I'm all about community and...stuff, so I figured I'd help out and work to make sure the preternatural and human gaps were bridged to make the most of a town-wide event."

She made a noncommittal noise. "I hate it when you logic me," she muttered, but in good nature. Madison was rarely in bad nature. It just wasn't her...nature.

Gabriel chuckled as he sat down on the armrest beside her. I briefly worried for the stability of my sofa, since he wasn't exactly a small guy. It seemed to be holding, though, so I tried to not worry about it further.

"What if we asked Dakota to give pony rides?" Vance suggested.

"That would be even easier than getting you into a dunking booth," I said sarcastically, pointedly ignoring his attempt to change my target.

He waved the hand without the glass. "Come on, isn't there something in the lore about vampires melting in water?"

I narrowed my eyes at him. "Yes, which is why there's a puddle of you in the bathroom after you shower all the, wait, never."

"She's logic-ing me now too," he grunted into his cup.

"You people have no town spirit," I moaned, tossing my notebook on the coffee table and getting to my feet. I took my empty glass into the kitchen as I muttered and mumbled and cursed at the lot of them while putting the cup in the sink.

A moment later, Madison followed me in. She leaned back against the counter and tilted her head with a smile. "You're not really upset, are you?"

I chuckled and rested against the fridge. "Of course not," I said. "Although you guys could be a little more helpful." With the boys still out in the living room, I took a long moment to look at my friend.

It had been years that we'd known each other, and she was practically a sister to me. Until she married, we had lived together in this house. It was kind of strange to not have her there anymore, although having Vance made it not as empty as it would've been. I had never expected to marry, but I always knew that she would move onto it at some point.

"Married life seems to be treating you well," I said. We still worked together so it wasn't like we didn't see each other, but it was still different. "Should I be expecting the pitter patter of little wolf pup paws any day now?" I grinned teasingly.

"Sadie," she chastised, but in a friendly way as she laughed and rolled her eyes. "We've only been married a few months. I'm still getting used to all the dirty socks."

I laughed in surprise. I had been expecting any number of comebacks, but for some reason, that one caught me off guard. "And all the fur?"

She waved a hand. "I've been used to that forever, although it being someone else's is new. Especially when it..." She hesitated and then laughed softly. "Yeah, well, it's still all taking some getting used to."

Peering across the kitchen at her, I figured I had a good idea what that stammer was about. "Things still going well with Chance?"

"They're great," she said with a flash of a smile. I knew

when she was lying, so I knew that she wasn't trying to cover up a problem. They really were all doing good. Well, more power to them, I figured. It wasn't my business what life in their bedroom was like. It might have seemed strange to me, but so many things were.

"Come on," I said, stepping forward and putting my hand on her shoulder. "I need your help talking the boys into cooperating with me…"

We walked back into the living room and took our seats. As she was settling down, Madison's jeans beeped. She pulled her phone from her pocket, looked at it, and smiled, then showed it to Gabe. He smiled too. I had a feeling what that was all about, but I wasn't going to say anything.

In quite a different show, Vance was frowning at his own phone.

"What's wrong?" I asked.

"I just read a headline about that new bill that started in the House," he said. With a soft scoffing sound, he turned off the screen and tossed it on the table.

"It's not the first time this has happened," I said, reaching out and putting my hand over his. This was perhaps the fourth or fifth time, I was losing track, that someone had proposed a bill to try and repeal Cameron's Law. "It will never make it out of committee. None of them have."

"People are worried, though," Madison chimed in. "You know we've been getting calls, although most are okay to vent at me. Some closer to D.C. are saying that this time feels different, though they have yet to be able to make clear in what way."

I frowned thoughtfully. "They always freak out whenever these happens. I don't blame them, but… It's in committee. It'll stay there. We have friends who make sure of it." Although even I had to admit that it seemed like there was a bit more uneasiness floating around about this one than usual. After a moment where we all sat in uncertain silence, I waved a hand. "We can't do anything now, but we can plan the town party. So, let's do it."

☾O☽

By the end of the night, Vance had agreed to see if anyone else at the station would be willing to take part. He further agreed that if Sam did, he would. Gabriel volunteered himself and the pack to handle all the meat and the BBQ.

Gabriel and Madison had just left when my phone rang.

I couldn't imagine anyone who'd be calling me so close to morning unless it was business, and my caller ID said it was D. I answered.

"Lucia got attacked." He didn't bother with any pleasantries, although it wasn't his style anyway.

"Tell me."

"We were on a job at St. Mary's cemetery and three whackjobs came out of the fucking greenery. I put their asses in the dirt, and they ran off. I took her to the Coven House, so the wardens could help protect her. She's okay, just shaken."

I pinched the bridge of my nose with a sigh. "I'll be right there."

After reporting quickly to Vance what was going on and where I was going, I headed out. I wasn't sure how long this would take, so I knew I might end up staying over at the Coven House. After all, vampires don't really like to get caught out in the sun while they're spending their day dead. It's just inconvenient.

The drive was quick, and Shayna greeted me at the door. She brought me into the more casual living room, rather than the formal 'receiving room,' where Lucia was sitting with her legs pulled up in an armchair. She had a cup of tea, and I was surprised that the coven kept any on hand. They did have non-vampire visitors at times, though. Meanwhile, D hovered in the corner like a specter of wrath.

She smiled slightly at me as I went to sit on the couch next to her chair. "How're you, Lucia?"

"I'm alright," she said. "It had been a little while and I'd begun to think the idiots had found a new pastime. This time, though, it was three. And plenty shouting their usual horrible things. The only small grace was that my client had already left so she wasn't there to be terrified out of her bloody wits. Seeing her mother rise again had been rough enough on the woman."

"They seemed a little more…determined than usual," D said. His arms were crossed over his broad chest as he leaned against the doorframe.

"I thought D was going to tear their heads from their shoulders," Lucia commented, and she didn't at all sound like she would've minded. She lifted her mug and took a long sip. I could hear her heart beating. It thudded louder than a normal heart should, and I knew that she was more shaken than she was letting on.

I looked up at him and nodded my appreciation. He nodded in return, seeming to understand what my silent gesture meant.

Turning back to Lucia, I patted her hand. "Will you be staying here tonight?"

She nodded. "I would rather not be alone tonight."

☾○☽

"You're insane. You know that, right?"

I stared at Cameron across the table. A plate was before him and a glass before me, but now both sat untouched as we stared one another down. He was unmoved by my shock and just kept smiling in that irrepressible, obnoxious way he had.

"You want to tell the whole wide fucking ignorant world that vampires and werewolves are real?" I asked again, sure that I hadn't heard him right.

"Yes!" He pounded his fist on the table. It almost broke. "Why not?"

I almost choked on my tongue. "WHY NOT?! Are you seriously asking that?" I paused and stared again. "Are you high? Is that what this is? Are you on all the things?" I could not imagine the substance that would make a shifter this high, but there had to be something.

With a growling huff, he pushed himself away from the table and started pacing the length of our small living room. "I'm not high, Sadie! I'm tired!" He ran his hands through his short blonde hair and then pulled on it. "I'm tired of hiding!"

"But, Cameron..." I began, feeling like I would cry if I had the tears. "You will come out of hiding in just enough time to be killed. At best, we'll just be laughed at. At worst..."

"Sadie, we can do this!" he went on, moving in front of me and kneeling. He took both of my cold hands in his, so warm, and I could feel the pounding of his heart. "Think about what our life could be if we could truly be free."

I bit my lip. "But, Cameron, it's so dangerous..."

He squeezed my hands. "Life is risk, Sadie," he said softly. "But what rewards if we succeed."

CHAPTER TWO

Acouple of nights later found me at the office. Lucia was recovered and back to work, and it was generally business as usual. For the most part, at least. Calls of concern about Congress were still coming in, and now I found myself often thinking about Cameron's friend. He was still a sitting congressman and remained a friend to me. We didn't talk so much as we had in those early weeks, but every now and then…

I finally decided that I needed to talk to him. I didn't want to be an alarmist, but there were too many alarms going off not to be. I got out my cell phone and dialed. He answered on the third ring.

"I was wondering when I'd be hearing from you," he said. I could hear both warmth and weariness in his voice.

"Hello, John," I said in a similar tone. "If you knew I'd be calling, you could have called me first." I didn't force him to answer that. "What do you know?"

He sighed. I heard the creaking of leather, like he was leaning back in a chair. "Not enough, frankly. That's why I haven't called." He answered the question I didn't ask him anyways. "My wife is going insane." His wife being a werewolf, though she still lived in Massachusetts. "I know that the same idiot has brought it forward who has brought forward most of the others, but they're saying something is different about this one. I'm not sure what yet, but enough people who'd know are saying it. Something about the language in the bill being different…being written better."

This wasn't good. "None of the others have gotten very far. Why should we think that this one will?"

"I can't answer that yet…" He trailed off in a way that would've made my stomach flip, if it still could. I grew anxious in other ways, though.

"Should I be nervous, John?"

"Yes."

When I hung up on that call, I felt colder than usual. I was almost in a daze as I got up and walked into the front room, although I forgot why when I saw the way D was staring at his phone. I hadn't even known that he and Lucia were back. Madison was beside him with a hand on his shoulder.

She looked up and saw me. "Cassandra has gone into labor. She's being taken to the hospital."

My eyes widened. The big event that had been freaking everyone out for months: how was a vampire going to deliver a baby?

"You're not driving," I declared to the slack-jawed man. My own haze lifted in an instant. "Man the office," I told Madison.

"Shouldn't that be woman the office?" she said.

I looked at her dryly. "Cancel Lucia's appointments if you can't find a backup. Call Dakota or Edward and see if they'd pitch in, otherwise, move the appointments." I hurried forward and put my arm around his shoulders as best I could—more like half around his mid-back—and then guided him out the door and into my car.

As he wasn't a man prone to excessive conversation, it was hardly surprising that he said nothing on the drive to the hospital. He just stared out the window with that same out-of-it expression, and who could blame him? Any father could lose their minds when they realized their wife—girlfriend, lover, whatever—was going into labor, but this was the most special of cases, and we all knew the risks were high.

☾○☾

Cassandra was likely to survive no matter what, vampires are pretty hardy, but the child was human... Who knew what might happen to it? We could only hope, or pray if so inclined, for the best.

Through some black magic, I did not get pulled over for speeding on the way. We were directed by a nurse at the counter who looked accustomed to such entries to maternity, and Jade and Shayna were in the waiting area. Shayna said nothing but turned and went to talk to the nurse at the counter, who instantly came out to take D.

Still, no one spoke. Vampires could be a remarkably silent bunch. Silent as the grave, one might say...if they were feeling punny.

"How was she?" I asked Jade.

The small Asian woman looked...uncharacteristically nervous. Although perfectly poised as always, there was a tightness around her dark eyes as she looked down the hall and then back at me. "Physically, she seemed as well as one might be. In pain, of course, but her body did nothing else that would alarm us. I don't know if a vampire's water could break, but in theory..." She trailed off thoughtfully. "Either way, it did not. Mentally, however, she was bouncing between her selves more from when it began to now than I have ever seen her do."

Shayna, far larger and more imposing than the coven leader, stood like a bodyguard. "She has made great progress for these months," she said. I noticed that her accent—she was born and raised in Israel—was thicker than usual, with anxiety she wasn't otherwise showing, I guessed. "But was like... She panicked."

"None can blame her," I said.

"No, certainly not," Shayna agreed flatly. I would've been concerned if she wasn't usually 'flat' emotionally. "But the panic seemed to make her…shatter. I do not think this for good, just for the moment. She will recover. We make sure of it."

Jade smiled, an economical gesture as always, and patted Shayna's hand where it curved around her arm. "We will make sure of it," she agreed.

With that, we all waited.

As I sat, there was much going through my mind. It wasn't like the phone call in my office was gone, but much of that space was filled with worry for Cass.

Even though we had all had months to adapt to it, I still found I could barely wrap my head around the idea. When I was turned, I gave up all ideas of having a child…and yet here we sat, waiting on a vampire to have a baby.

It made me wonder…but no, I knew this was a once-in-the-world chance. To anyone's best guess, it was only possible because of Cassandra's broken mind. And since she was being pieced together, cautiously, it would not happen again.

"Hello?" a young man said, and we all turned our attention to him. I smelled the faint trace of forest and dog on the air, and I knew him for a werewolf. He was tall and looked strong enough, and I knew why he was there.

"Madison sent you?" I asked.

"Yes, ma'am," he said. I detected a hint of the South on his voice. "I'm here to help once dawn comes, what with the parents and all."

I nodded. It had been agreed once we knew the baby would be human that they'd need non-vampire help. Madison had been willing to help arrange it before, but now as pack alpha, she was even better set up for it.

Jade looked him over like a predator appraising its prey,

but I knew she was just evaluating him to take care of her vampires. She could be very protective. To the young wolf's credit, he stood and took it without flinching.

"You are qualified to take care of a newborn?" she asked after a moment.

"Helped raised four half-siblings, ma'am, before I moved here," he replied. "Was fifteen when the first was born. Mrs. Raines wouldn't have chosen me otherwise."

It was still weird hearing her called that, but obviously, I kept it to myself.

"Have a seat then," Jade waved at the chair still left empty because Shayna would not sit down. Really, none of us needed to sit because of what we were, but we were not immune to discomfort. Sometimes, I thought Shayna preferred it.

❰○❱

With the young man—Jason—now waiting with us, we all...waited. It seemed like forever before D came out. He wore scrubs, which looked odd on him, but I knew that Cassandra's delivery could only have been a C-section. We all knew that from the start, since a vampire body would not deliver naturally.

He smiled. We all relaxed. "It's..." Stumbling, choked with emotion that would never be shown in tears, he caught himself. "I have a son."

We all grinned. I got up and crossed the waiting room with preternatural speed, hugging him with a strength I knew a vampire could handle. When I pulled back, I looked up at him.

"And Cassandra is well?"

He nodded. I hadn't let go of him yet. "She's good," he said. "She settled into Anne when surgery began, but as soon as he was out, she was Cass again and has been since. Vampires having no blood pressure made it easy, or so the doctor said. No one can figure out how the baby survived. He's a miracle, they say."

I hugged him again. "He is at that."

☾○☽

By the next night, D and Cassandra were still at the hospital. They would remain for three nights, one more than usual because of the unusual birth. Shayna made sure that the curtains were suitably thick, and Jason remained there for every daylight hour.

They named him Evan. He was small but healthy.

Edward was pitching in to cover for D while he remained at the hospital. It was Madison's night off, and the office was quiet. I planned to go see the baby (again) with Vance once we were both off work later, but for now, I had an office to attend to.

The small television in my office was on while I worked, and the news came on. I didn't pay it much mind, because I had plenty else to think about, until certain words caught my attention.

"This latest attempt by the anti-preternatural component of congress has left committee and hearings will again begin," the reporter said.

My head snapped up so fast, I almost broke my neck. Thankfully, I couldn't have my heart stop or I would've died at the pronouncement. My rallying cry for days had been that what had just happened *wouldn't happen*. They kept talking, getting into the history of Cameron's Law, talking about Cameron, even bringing me up, but I didn't care. All I knew was that my best shield had suddenly been taking away.

For the first time in all these years, a bill to push us back into the shadows was gaining traction. The horror knew no bounds.

The report suddenly went to an interview with Frederick Hughes. He had been my nemesis during the legality trials and just about ever since. He couldn't keep his trap shut about the preternatural.

Would the man never go away?

"I'm just glad that the good people now in Congress are seeing the wrongs of those before," he went on, ignoring that it was mostly the same Congress as before. It hadn't been *decades* yet. "This time, I'm sure that the right path will be chosen—"

I threw the remote at the television and cracked the screen. It sparked once in its death throes, and then both lines of the telephone system began to ring in mourning.

Grabbing up the phone, I answered and cycled through calls as best I could.

There were already anti-preternatural demonstrations breaking out all over the country. Like it was...organized.

I felt lightheaded. Which was weird for a vampire, but every call, I either learned some bit of news that made it worse or people wanting to know what I knew. That was very little, and I finally had to ignore the calls coming in so I could make one going out.

"John," I began, feeling tight through my whole body.

"I know!" he replied, sounding almost as upset as I was. I was sure his wife was panicking in his ear, wondering just where she could go now that would be safe.

"There's hearings," I almost shouted. I only restrained myself at the last moment because I knew my vampire volume could burst his ears, even over the phone. "You need to get my voice in there. You have to get me time before congress."

I could hear him take a long breath. "I'm going to, Sadie. I promise. None of us saw this coming, and now we're all scrambling. I still don't know what the hell is going on, and I'm trying to keep my wife from tying a bedsheet rope out the window of our house."

Pressing my lips together, I forced myself to calm down. "I know, John... I'm sorry."

"It's all right, just... I'm working on it. I promise."

He hung up, and I stared at my broken television. We were going to have to do it all again. I could see the past rolling out before me like a bad daydream. We would have to speak before congress, plead for our lives, protest and petition, but now the stakes were so much higher.

We couldn't let it pass out of the House. It had to be stopped where it stood.

We had to do it all again.

CHAPTER THREE

Being a vampire had its benefits, like not sweating.

I came up to the podium. The men and women before me weren't used to convening at night, but obviously, there was a special circumstance to be made here. They looked at me without any clear attempt to hide their feelings, which ranged from disgust to curiosity to disbelief. None of these were surprising.

They knew what I was going to say, and most thought I was crazy.

I was crazy, just not for the reasons they thought.

"Thank you for your time and listening tonight," I began. I tried to project strength and calm while I was freaking out and waiting for a Van Helsing with a stake around every corner. "My name is Sadie Stanton. You have all heard of me by now. I come before you today to tell you that I am..." Even I couldn't say the next part without hesitation. This was it. This was the point of no return. "I am a vampire."

The hall broke out in a quiet din, ranging from murmuring to outright laughter. I waited until it quieted down.

"None of you believe me. If I were in your positions, I would not believe me either. I, however, have the benefit of this existence. I was born in nineteen-eighteen and turned during the Great Depression." Again, the noise. Again, I waited. I lifted the device on the podium in front of me. "This is what they use to hear the heartbeats of babies while still in the womb. It will project my heartbeat loud enough for you all the hear."

Looks were exchanged.

I made a show to demonstrate turning it on and then placed it on my chest.

The silence was deafening.

Standing that way, I let them all realize what that meant. Then I offered anyone who wished to come up and try it themselves the chance to do so, and all their heartbeats could be heard. I opened the top of my shirt just enough to show that no device prevented it working and let others hold it to my chest. Still nothing. Some felt for my pulse on my bare neck or bare wrist themselves.

It was like being a test subject for science, or a sideshow freak, but I allowed it.

When all were satisfied, which took forever, they one by one returned to their seats. "Do I have your attention now?" I asked softly, just loud enough to be heard.

This time, no one laughed.

《○》

Once I had gotten all the calls sorted out enough to escape, I left the office. I put on the answering service and made a break for it. I was sure that she had already heard the news, but I had to talk to her about it in person. So, I headed for the pack house, where Madison had moved to when she married Gabe.

When I got there, I found another car in the drive besides theirs, but it was common for other pack members to be there. So I parked and went up to the door and knocked. The question of the car was answered when Chance answered. He looked fit to tear someone apart until he saw that it was me and nodded. Saying nothing, he stepped back and let me enter. His demeanor made me frown, because it seemed like something other than just watching the news.

I walked into the living room, where I found Madison

sitting on the couch—or rather perched on the edge of it. It was reminiscent of going to see Lucia, only there was a half-faded bruise on her cheekbone and eye, and tears covering her cheeks. Gabriel was sitting beside her with his arm around her shoulders. Chance moved past me and sat on her other side, his hand over hers.

"What happened?" I asked, momentarily forgetting why I had come. I saw blood and bruises on the knuckles of both men and felt dread sinking through me.

"We were attacked," Gabriel said. Chance still looked angry, perhaps too much to talk. He leaned his head against hers, and she returned the gesture.

"When… Where…" I was dumbfounded, like I should somehow have known.

"Walking through town on our way home. We're so near the center, so why not walk when we can?" Gabe asked, his smile bitter and wry. "Chance and I had stopped for a moment… Fuck, I don't even remember why now. She walked on ahead. Four came out from the street side, you know, where the trees are. They were on her in a moment. But she fought like hell and had one of them on the ground before Chance and I caught up." He kissed her temple with obvious pride.

"All the usual slurs," Madison said softly, turning dull blue eyes at me. "It felt like back in the day. What they shouted at Cameron and I when we were out. Monster. Abomination. Hell hound. Vile creature. Name it, they said it." She raised one shaking hand to brush at her cheek.

"We already went to the police and made a report," Gabe said. "They got away. I wanted to make sure she was okay, otherwise I might have chased after them."

Now I could see in a bit of shadow that the corner of his mouth was split and had dried blood around it. I imagined there were other injuries, but I tried not to think through it too much as I wondered why Vance hadn't told me. He knew

Madison was practically my sister...but that was for later.

"Madison, I'm so sorry," I whispered. "All of you, I'm... glad you're okay, but... Fuck!" I gripped my ponytail and pulled on my hair. The sharp pain in my scalp helped me get my shit together for a moment. "It's the bill."

"We saw," she said quietly. "We fighting again?" Her eyes glistened with tears, but I saw her brother's spirit in them. No, it was *her* spirit, but I had seen that fire in them both. They were not the kind to be put down, or bullied, or threatened. I could never get either of them to do anything they didn't choose to. "Sadie. We're fighting again."

I nodded. "Yes. We're fighting again."

She sniffled and then visibly swallowed as she nodded. "Good," she said, though her voice was still thick with emotion. "I've already put the pack on a sort of...buddy system. No wolf is to be alone, including the one at the hospital and then Coven House. We told Jade about it, and she'll do the same."

Suddenly, I wondered if anyone needed me for anything anymore.

"Good," I said, nodding.

I stayed a little while longer to assure myself that she was indeed alright, that they all were. They were family.

As I left, I checked my phone and realized that Vance wasn't in trouble: I had five missed calls. I called him back as I sat in my car in Madison's driveway. It started to rain as I rambled my panic at him, and I thought maybe the sky was crying for me.

☾ ○ ☽

I didn't want to go home, because I knew I'd be there alone. However, I didn't want to intrude on Madison and her boys any longer either. Vance said I could come to the station house, so I did.

"I've been talking to other cops in other areas of the country, and Jackson has called about some," he told me as we sat in the breakroom and he held my hands. "It's not just here. There are reports of violence and hate crimes all over the country, already. It's happening fast, honey. Like…"

"Like it was planned," I said quietly, since I had already had that thought.

He nodded. I could see he was keeping his face as impassive as possible, neutral, but his eyes were worried.

After he got back to work, I called John. Again. I had a feeling we'd be in lockstep, and his news was no more reassuring. It seemed there was some power to this movement and more than just the usual bigots. John didn't know who, but he was trying to find out.

When Vance's shift was over, we found a pair of werewolves on our doorstep. Our bodyguards during the day.

I thanked them profusely, but I still felt such melancholy in my heart.

This time was going to be so much harder and more painful.

We had so much more to lose.

Chapter Four

'Monster' was scrawled across our door in dripping red paint.

Madison and I stood staring at it. We hardly could be surprised, but that didn't make it any less horrifying. "I don't suppose any of us thought it would be easy," she said quietly. "Still, it would have been nice."

Stepping forward, I knelt down. "It would've been nice," I said quietly, finding a handful of papers thrown at the door. Cheap paper. It looked like someone had printed it at home and then used a copier, a cheap one. Everything was smudged, including the stupid horror movie script.

"Vampires shouldn't be given legal rights. They should be given the stake." That was the line at the top, and more followed. At the bottom, it read, "The League of Humans Against Vampires."

I held it up and showed Madison. "Hatred can organize," I said.

No, of course this was never going to be easy. But it would've been nice.

❨◯❩

I began my campaign the next night and although I did go into the office, most of my hours for that night and the next were engulfed in this pursuit.

What would my business matter if I had to go into hiding?

Madison and I took to the internet. There were petitions to organize and peaceful protests, demonstrations, to put together. She handled most of that because she was more savvy at social media than I was. Amidst my worry for my friends and my own husband, out there on the street to purposely seek trouble, I had to worry about Facebook and Twitter.

I called John a lot, but he didn't know anything yet. What he did know was that people were actively stonewalling him, because he was an advocate. It pissed him off, as well it should, but he was determined. I asked Bill, the demon lawyer of the agency, to keep in touch with any friends he had in D.C. An ear to the ground, so to speak.

I talked to everyone and anyone. I chased people down by any means necessary, but I never went out alone.

We were lucky. No one had been killed...yet.

I was going to do every damn thing possible to make sure it stayed that way.

☾O☽

My phone was ringing when I became conscious the next night. The sound instantly made me feel like my stomach had fallen to the bottom of my feet, and I almost couldn't reach for it. Dread filled me. For two nights, I'd been waiting for another call, another attack. There had to be one. It wasn't done.

They were coming for us.

I answered it anyway, because I couldn't *not*.

"Someone attacked Lorelei," Madison told me. "A wolf at the hospital told me. Edward is there. Dakota has been called, but her and Sam are about an hour's drive away."

Not the way Dakota was driving, I imagined.

"I'll go there." We hung up.

Vance was just coming to. As a younger vampire, it took him a little longer. I told him what was going on.

"Did she know if there was a report?"

"I didn't ask," I replied, since thinking like a cop wasn't something I did.

"I'll check in with the station. If not, I'll come there."

I got dressed quickly and hurried to the hospital, a place I was coming to see far too often of late. She was still in a room in the emergency room, and I was directed there. When I entered, I found her sitting up in bed and Edward sitting beside her. She had her arm in a sling and those white butterfly stickers over cuts on her cheekbone.

She smiled weakly. "You didn't have to come down here."

I returned the expression as I moved to her bed. "Of course I did," I said. "You're family now." Sitting on the edge, I felt guilty. She was human. She wouldn't recover from this as fast as the rest of it, and she shouldn't have been a part of it. This shouldn't have been happening to any of us. "I'm so sorry."

"It's not your fault," she said. "But...I definitely never imagined something like this happened. If I ever imagined some kind of hate crime, I didn't think it would be the species of my boyfriend that did it..."

"What happened?" I asked gently.

"A lot of shouting." She frowned, staring at her feet. She was still in her street clothes, but her shoes were off. "Something like...monster-lover. I was just walking out of the vet's, having dropped a dog off. They hit me, knocked me around the side of the building, and did all this. There were two. One of them said something like... Something about sending a message?" She sighed. "I caught one between the legs with my knee and hammered the other one to the bridge of the nose, then I hauled ass away."

"Good for you," I said sincerely. "Have you seen the police?"

She nodded. "They called them from here. Some uniform came and took my statement and description."

I heard shouting down the hall.

Edward looked at the door and then back at me. "Dakota."

Hopping off the bed, I rushed out of the room. I found her storming down the hallway and was somewhat surprised that she wasn't in some sort of animal form. (My guess about her driving had been right, however. That definitely had not taken an hour.)

"What the fuck happened?!" she demanded when she saw me.

"She was hurt, but she's okay now," I said, holding my hands out. That was when I saw Sam beside her, holding her arm.

"It's not going to do her any good to have you storming in there like a tornado, Anneliese," she said quietly. So quietly that I may not have heard her if not for my vampire's hearing. The use of Dakota's real name—her birth name from the 1600s—seemed to calm her down, and she blew out a hard breath.

"She was attacked?" she asked, this time much calmer. "Like we were hearing on the news? LOHAV is kicking up its heels again and landing them on our faces?"

"Yes," I said. I wouldn't lie to her. "We're going to do all we can. You know that."

Her eyes were tight and she pressed her lips together, but she nodded. Then she blew past me, Sam in tow, and went into Lorelei's room.

I was left standing in the hallway. I considered going

back in, but I didn't feel it appropriate now.

"Hey." It was Vance. I turned to see him standing in the hall, his hands in the pockets of his pants as he watched me.

"She said the police already took her report," I said quietly.

"I came anyway," he said. "They have my number if they need me." He opened his arms, and I ran into them, sobbing without any moisture at all. Just emotion and sound. My body still remembered how, after all these long years.

"They're coming after us," I whispered into his chest. "Coming after those around me."

He nodded, a slight movement of his head against mine. "They want to break you, because you rallied everyone before. They don't want you doing it again. Look how fast these have happened. They want you distracted."

Pulling back, I looked up at him. "I didn't do it alone last time. It wasn't even my damn idea!"

"You're not alone now either, are you?"

I sighed. "So, what do I do? How do I keep people safe?"

He looked at me like he couldn't believe I had to ask the question. "You fight this shit, and you win. We'll be safe when we stuff them all back in those dark holes they crawled out of."

With a sigh, I buried my face against him. Not having to breathe had its benefits. I wondered if I had the strength to do it all again, but then, did I really have a choice? Did I want them to win? Did I want to go back to pretending I was not who I was? Only this time, I wouldn't have any cover. Before, no one knew my face so I could do what I wanted under whatever story I wanted. Now? It seemed the whole country knew who I was. Could I hide again?

I heard footsteps behind us and pulled away from Vance enough to turn around. It was Sam. She came up to us with an apologetic half-smile. "I'm sorry to interrupt, but y'all are in the middle of the hallway."

"What is it, Sam?" Vance asked his partner with a tired smile.

"They're gonna discharge Lorelei tonight," she said. "She's banged up but nothing requires admittance, so we'll be taking her home in a few hours." She turned to Vance. "I was due off for the rest of the night, but if you need me to come in, I will."

He shook his head. "Unless we find a way to be everywhere at once, I think I can handle the evening. You keep Dakota from breaking everyone's necks."

Sam nodded and patted me on the shoulder before returning to the room.

Vance drove me to the coven house, then went to work.

☾O☽

"Isn't it beautiful?" Cameron asked, grinning at me.

We sat in front of the television, watching the news video of the 'preternatural sit-in' that took place on the steps of Capitol Hill earlier that day. A whole host of preternatural beings, some in their human forms and others in animal form, just sitting on the steps. No vampires in this one since it was daytime, but the sprawl of wolves and tigers and falcons made an impact.

"Do you think this will accomplish anything more than getting more graffiti on our door and pamphlets scattered in the hall?" I asked quietly, thoughtfully. It was an impressive sight, that could not be denied, but...I was filled with dread.

He had made me a believer. I wanted the same end that he wanted, but the risks were terrifying. I didn't want to see anyone hurt, especially those around me.

Cameron put his arm around my shoulders and pulled

me close. "It'll work," he said. "It will be great."

Somehow, I was put in mind of a line from a movie. I couldn't remember the exact line or the movie, but something about stopping the dreamers before they kill us with their dreams. That worried me now, but I also remembered that safe lives were not always lives worth living. It was perhaps worth the risk.

Or so I hoped.

Chapter Five

Two agonizing nights more.

Silence on all the fronts where I wanted noise, and noise on all the fronts where I wanted silence. The one upside was that there were no more attacks, but the downside to even that was that I was constantly *waiting* for one. I lived in terror every conscious moment of getting a call that something had happened to Vance while on the job, or to the new baby, or Madison again, or... I could think of a thousand scenarios and they all plagued me.

I stared at my phone waiting for John or Bill to call. I watched the news, even though I knew I shouldn't.

Nothing. Nothing... Nothing!

Then, around half past ten that second night, my phone did ring. The chirping of my cell phone nearly made me leap out of my seat like a startled cat and flop over on the floor.

Grabbing it, I saw Bill's number.

"Hello?!"

"Sadie," he said. "I found out who's really behind this bill. And you're never going to believe it..."

《○》

It was a stupid, stupid idea. But there I was. Sitting outside the house of Congresswoman Tory Whitmer, representative for the state of Connecticut. She didn't live far from Adelheid, actually, and she had before been an advocate for us. This helped a great deal to explain why the power of the bill was hiding behind the others and John kept getting stonewalled. She didn't want anyone to know she had swapped loyalties.

She was home for the weekend, D.C. being only a few hours' drive from here. The lights were on in her house, so I knew she was home and awake.

I hadn't told Vance I was going there, because he would have told me it was a bad idea. Because it was. He would have been right, but there I was anyway.

Sam, on the other hand, was an ally. She helped me piece together something that had been kept pretty damned quiet in the past year, but that I was almost certain was fueling this now. I was hoping to use it to my advantage and turn the tide back our way, because I was desperate. My friends were being attacked at an alarming rate, and the anti-preternatural hate wave was growing by the moment.

If I didn't shove my foot in this woman's door, hearings could well end without our voice and our lives could be revoked.

So I walked up to her door, and I knocked. In so safe a neighborhood, she was willing to open the door the length of her burglar chain. Seeing me, she tried to shut it again, but I did just what I meant to do and shoved my foot in. "Please, Congresswoman!" I called. "Just please!"

"I have nothing to say to you, Miss Stanton," she returned, trying to flatten my foot, but I would not be budged, and I was way stronger.

"I know about your daughter!"

She stopped pushing but didn't say anything. She stared at me through the size eight-and-a-half gap, and I stared right back.

Taking her silence as a good step, I went on with a touch less volume to my desperation. "I know about your daughter, ma'am. I know that Ally was killed by that experimental cat thing that got loose almost a year ago. If you'll remember, it was my wedding reception that got crashed."

"I'm aware," she said tightly.

"Is that why you wrote that bill and let that idiot present it in the House?" I implored her with my tone and my eyes. "You would kill us all?"

She looked down. "It's gone too far."

I stared at her, even if she wouldn't look back. "Yes, our terrible agenda into supermarket shopping and hairdresser visits. Ma'am, I know you must be hurting. I... I can only imagine your pain. I never lost a child, but I did watch the man I love beaten to death right in front of me."

Now, her eyes met mine.

"Please, just let us talk."

"Fine," she finally relented, opening the door to permit my entrance.

The house sounded empty, aside from her and I. I followed her into a dimly lit but clean and fairly comfortable living room. It was a small house compared to what I'd expected, but then, what did I know?

I sat on the couch, and she sat in the armchair.

"You have one chance, but I'm not inclined to be pleased with you after stopping by so late at night without invitation or desire," she said tightly.

"I don't blame you, Congresswoman," I replied, holding up my hands. "Please understand for my part, I'm fighting for my life. The traction this bill has gained has increased violence against my people to levels not seen for years, and several among them have been my friends and family. We're terrified."

"I've heard on the news," she said, looking down at her hands in her lap. Despite the late hour, she still wore day clothes. Not the kind of thing she'd have worn at work, but not a nightgown or anything like that.

"I am so sorry for your daughter, I really am," I said and meant it. I was.

She lifted one nicely manicured hand and rubbed her eyes. "We were...estranged at the time it happened. She had been into so much trouble over the years, and I grew so weary of it, and I told her as much. Such a fight." I could hear the emotion in her voice, even as she covered her eyes and rubbing her forehead. "We were so distanced, and she had her father's last name, my ex, and she was considered so...unimportant when she died." She paused, choking up. "The news didn't even make the connection between she and I. And that 'cat thing' was so much more important." She shivered. "I wanted to reconnect...but then she died, and I never had a chance to fix it."

I listened patiently. "I'm sorry for that," I said again. "But it was not the fault of us all that it happened. It wasn't even us who started that. *Humans* ran Pre-Tech and made that thing, not us. The media wasn't our fault either. I know you want someone to pay, someone to blame, but please don't punish all of us for your grief. I'm begging you. You were an ally to us in the past. You believed we were people and had a right to live. Please don't turn your back on us now. Don't compound your daughter's death by adding to the toll. Help me turn this back around."

Lowering her hand, she let slightly bloodshot eyes fall on mine. If I'd been breathing, I would have held my breath.

☾O☽

Congresswoman Whitmer returned to D.C. on Sunday.

We were given time on the floor Monday night.

It was a rather strange caravan making our way down to D.C. Monday morning. Vance remained home to keep things in order, as did Gabriel for his pack. Madison and I, along with Chance, drove in one car. I was in the back under a blanket, since it was daytime. Behind us were Agent Lang and Nykk Marlowe. We had four slots for speaking. Of this group, Chance would not be. He was just there for Madison.

We were kept outside in the hall while each of us spoke. I was to go last so I got to sit nervously on a hard bench and watch as first Jackson went in, talking about working for this federal government as a pyrokinetic. He came out looking wearied. Nykk patted his shoulder as she went in, speaking of being a human touched by preternatural—and not in a good way—but how she would live and work with no one else. She spoke of advocating for the victims of anti-preternatural violence.

She wasn't a woman commonly inclined to smile, but she offered a faint one to me when she came out and sat beside Jackson.

Madison went in, and I knew she'd speak about her brother. She was crying when she came back out. I gave her my phone, which I had been using to text Vance while waiting. Chance had been with me, but we weren't much for small talk, and I didn't bother trying once he started pacing while Madison was in there.

"Bring the house down, Sadie," she whispered to me just before I went in.

It was perhaps the longest walk of my life, worse than the last time I'd been there. This time, they all knew that I was what I said I was. Did they judge me more now than they did before? I didn't know, and I couldn't look at anyone's face as I made my way to the podium and was introduced to speak.

"You all know who I am by now," I said as I lifted my head and looked at the sea of faces, growing blurry in my anxiety. "It has been some years since I stood in this same spot and spoke to you. There are a few new faces, but most of the same ones I met before. I am sure you remember all I said.

"You have heard from my friends and family before me. I'm sure there isn't much that I can say that they have not said, but it is important enough to bear repeating." I paused there and looked at the piece of paper before me, where I had written down my thoughts about what I was going to say. "We exist." I looked up again.

"You have now known for years that we are real. We have been living among you, in hiding, for centuries because of the fear that we would be killed. That fear grew paramount when we tried to walk out of hiding. And that fear was realized for some of us. As I am sure you have also heard. I would not have those dark days upon my kind again, in either form.

"We have the right to live like anyone else. If we commit a crime, we are to be punished, but I will not and will never hold that simply walking the Earth is enough to say we have done wrong. I own a business. I serve the public. My husband is a cop. I am married. We pay a mortgage—too much for it, I'm sure." This brought a few quiet laughs from the room. "We pay taxes. We are...boring.

"All we want is to not be driven back into the shadows. All we want is to not be killed for walking down the street. Why is that really so much to ask? Why are we *really* to be feared? Do I write checks in a threatening manner? Do I crawl along the ceiling of the supermarket? Is the money made from my business that goes to pay your salaries really so bloodied and evil? It is not, and I do not, and I am not.

"I am a vampire. I am no threat to any of you. I ask only to be allowed to have my life, such as it is, left intact and left alone. The only radical theory I propose is one of life. The only revolution I suggest is to walk the Earth, unshackled and unharmed.

"Yes, I am a vampire. I am also a person. I have family. I love. I feel pain. I feel fear. I don't want to hurt anyone. I just want to be allowed to exist. Please, I don't deserve a death sentence. Is that really asking for so much? I don't think it is. I hope that you all will agree when you go to vote on this proposal. Thank you."

There was a quiet round of applause as I left the podium and walked from the room. If I had hoped for a thunderous standing ovation like in the movies, I would have been disappointed, but I had not thought that would happen.

Madison met me at the door and hugged me. She cried.

We left then, because there was nothing more we could do. I knew that Congresswoman Whitmer would push for a vote. We had spoken. The stonewalling would end. It had to go to vote now and let it be determined whether to die there or live on in the Senate. If it lived, our fight would be that much harder.

❲O❳

"We won! We did it, Sadie!" Cameron nearly vibrated out of his skin as we walked down the Bostonian street beneath flickering street lamps that needed more funding.

"It's not signed yet," I pointed out, although I was smiling. I knew that it was as good as done. It had passed a vote in both halves of congress, and the president had already stated that were it to do so, he'd put it into law. I did not believe he would make any eleventh-hour changes of heart and try to veto it.

The Preternatural Rights Act would pass.

"Don't be such a pessimist, woman," he laughed, taking my hand and kissing it.

"You Cameron St John?"

The question came from behind us. It was not a voice that either of us recognized, and we turned.

There were three.

"Can I help you?" Cameron asked, but his joviality was already gone. None of these faces looked too friendly. They smelled human, though, so I was sure we could be okay. I just didn't want the trouble. This was supposed to be our night.

It happened fast. Faster than I could have expected. Silver. Two of them were on me, and one on Cameron. I could not see what happened to him. I knew that they were beating me with silver, but I couldn't see weapons.

I threw one, but the other drove a fist into my side that hurt way more than it should have. I spun on that one, but I already felt the silver in my bloodstream. Like poison. I staggered, and a fist to the face drove me to the ground, then they were on me.

I heard Cameron call my name, then I heard nothing.

☾O☽

The next night, we all hovered around our phones. I didn't even trust to put my cell in my pocket, lest I miss the ringing.

We were all working. I knew that the House would be voting that day, although it took place at night. I wasn't sure why, but it was. So we waited. We tried to work. It didn't really go all that well. Madison came into my office every five minutes to ask if I'd heard anything.

Finally, my phone rang.

It was John.

EPILOGUE

Fourth of July

The town green of Adelheid, Connecticut, was alive—with people and big outdoor lights to illuminate the night for the humans in attendance. We all had much reason to celebrate, and all the inclination to do so. Even those who might not have shown up for the party before we there now, because the House bill had been voted down.

Suddenly losing steam, anti-preternatural violence had retreated again.

"How the fuck did you ever talk him into it?" Dakota asked as she came up behind me, looking at Vance sitting on the bench of the dunk booth. "And how did you convince my girlfriend to go along with it too? Has the police force entirely lost their minds?"

"Dakota, you have no sense of the whimsical." I smirked sidelong at her.

She returned the expression. "Seriously, when have you ever thought that the word 'whimsical' fit me?"

I made an act of considering. "Never. Although it was proposed that we ask if you wanted to give pony rides."

Her eyes widened and brows rose. "Who do I need to hit for even giving such a suggestion out loud?"

To that, I laughed at her. "Think I'll ever tell?" I started walking away.

"I could make you talk!" she called after me.

"No, you couldn't," I declared, turning around just in time to see her dog (Buster) come flying out of nowhere. He made one of those amazing athletic leaps his breed can achieve and caught me firm on the chest, knocking me onto my back. My face was sodden just moments later as more dog kisses than I could possibly count were slobbered on me.

Even a vampire could barely ward off such affection.

"He could," Dakota said with a grin as she knelt beside me and didn't try to help.

"Dakota!" I called, getting dog tongue in my mouth for my trouble. I finally got my hands on his chest and held him off.

Finally, she came to my rescue with a whistle, and Buster bounded off. She took up his leash again just as I saw Edward and Lorelei leaning over me. She was smiling sympathetically, and he offered me a hand up.

Seeing her arm sling still gave me a twinge of guilt, but she seemed in good spirits.

Once again on my feet, I could see Gabriel and Chance manning the large grill the pack had brought to the green. I couldn't hear what they were saying over the conversational din, but it looked like there was disagreement about the best way to cook the meat. Boys and their meat, it seemed, were the same no matter the species.

Perhaps shifters, with their strong carnivorous tendencies, were even fiercer.

Suddenly, a squeal from my left brought me around. I saw Madison pushing through the crowd, but not toward me. I followed her line of sight and saw D first, with Cassandra with him and something in her arms.

Two-week-old Evan already had wide-open blue eyes and more keen interest than a newborn had any right to. Cassandra had the little one in one of those baby wrap things that looked more like a way to string a person up by their ankles than carry an infant, but she'd obviously figured it out.

"We can't stay long," D said, hovering protectively. He had been back to work, although part-time.

"But we wanted to say hello and introduce Evan to his town family," Cass said. She smiled with that airy look she usually did, although there was something different about her. I eyed her for a moment, wondering if she wasn't, you know, Cassandra. She seemed to see my wondering, because she said, "It's me. The others are...quiet again."

I smiled and patted her on the shoulder. "Enjoy your time. There's a cooler over there by the stage with some vampire fare."

D smiled slightly. "Thanks, Sadie."

Putting my hand on his shoulder, I moved back into the crowd. I heard one of the uniformed officers I knew by face but not by name calling encouragement to the one throwing the baseball, trying to get Vance in the water. I stopped to watch for a moment and was apparently bad luck, because he dropped a moment later.

I laughed. I wouldn't hear the end of this for a while, but the dunked cat look made it worth it.

A group of pack children were hovering around Buster, and he was bathing all their faces as thoroughly as he had mine. Dakota was even smiling, and I saw Nykk's younger sister in there with the group while Nykk and Jackson watched with their own smiles.

There didn't seem to be a face anywhere in this crowd that I didn't know. I saw reporters from the *Adelheid Chronicle*, not even looking like they were bothering to take notes. Posey Kai was there with her vampire, holding his arm and walking him around, narrating the festivities he couldn't see.

Abby had even been dragged out, looking a little less morose than usual as she hung out with Quintus, Jade, and Shayna. D and Cassandra were moving to join them, and I couldn't help but laugh when they let Quintus hold the baby. The little human infant seemingly vanished in the big hands and big arms of the massive vampire.

A sodden Vance was dragging Sam to the dunk booth while she tried to dig her feet in, and Madison was jumping up trying to see over the tall, broad shoulders of the boys at the grill. I could almost hear her demanding to know when the food would be ready. While she was distracting them, a pack teenager came around from behind and grabbed a steak. The look on his face at the burn was hysterical as he kept from crying out, running off to eat his illicit gains with his pack alphas none the wiser.

I smiled and looked at them all. These... These were my people. The vampires, and the shapeshifters, and the psychics, and the fae, and the humans. They were all mine. It had nothing to do with their species, but everything to do with *this*.

We were family. We were a community.

We were Adelheid.

Author's Note

"Endings are hard. Any chapped-ass monkey with a keyboard can poop out a beginning, but endings are impossible. You try to tie up every loose end, but you never can. The fans are always gonna bitch. There's always gonna be holes. And since it's the ending, it's all supposed to add up to something. I'm telling you, they're a raging pain in the ass."

~ *Supernatural*, Season 5 Finale

Chuck was right. Endings are hard. They're hard for all of what he said, but they're also hard because good-byes are hard. This is the final book in the Blood Rights Series, where the first version of the first book started nearly twenty years ago for me. I have written these characters in all sorts of different ways and places, not just in this series, and I love them like they're real.

To me, they are.

By the time I wrote the first version of this particular story, however, they were also tired. It had been many years and many stories with many events and traumas and craziness in between. Their voices in that creative corner of my mind were ready for a break, so I gave it to them. This concludes this series. It started with Sadie, introducing you all, dear readers, to the world with Cameron's Law. It's now ended with Sadie, fighting for their rights to be themselves. Refusing to be pushed back into myth and shadow.

The series ultimately ended up having a much stronger theme of 'equal rights' and the fight for it than I'd originally planned, but I haven't minded that. In fact, I'm proud of it. As someone who has felt on the outside for many reasons over the years, equal rights for everyone has always been dear to my heart. I've modeled the struggle here in this series from the world, from the country (the U.S., where I live), and from within my own heart.

In a lot of ways, this series was like the quote, "All you do is sit down at a typewriter and open a vein." (Attribution and exact phrasing are hazy, but the idea is there.) These stories came about kind of like that, if you don't mind a rather gross metaphor, but these are vampire books.

This isn't the end *completely*, however. It's the end of this arc, but the world of Adelheid will live on. It will live beyond Adelheid. It will live on in Hunter's Point, ME, when the Vic Glass Paranormal Mysteries Series comes out. It will live on aboard a space station, when we meet the eternal characters (and the descendants of the not-eternal ones) two hundred years in the future and out in space. It will live on in a series planned to revisit these characters during points in history...

That's one of the beauties of paranormal characters like these—so many options!

Hey, we might even return to modern-day Adelheid later on. For now, though, these guys are just going to live their bizarrely normal lives as preternatural beings alongside us.

I hope you've enjoyed reading their stories as much as I've enjoyed writing them, and we'll see you around again soon...

If you want to know more about the town of Adelheid, the people who live in it, and the lore I chose to use when writing these preternatural species, you can check out my series wiki at wiki.authorkbthorne.com.

Sincerely,

K. B. Thorne, June 2021

ABOUT THE AUTHOR

Born a Connecticut Yankee in nobody's court, K. B. Thorne grew up to brave snow and talk fast.

She started reading when she was three and never looked back, soon frequently falling asleep with a book under her cheek. At eleven, she discovered *Night Mare* by Piers Anthony and entered the world of grown-up fantasy fiction. As you can guess, it was all over from there. She started writing at fourteen, then met vampires as a teenager and the concept for what would become Adelheid (now the Blood Rights Series) was soon born. Mia Darien followed a few years later, and the books were released.

However, K. B. is also a third-generation Trekkie. Somewhere in a vault at Paramount is a very angry letter written by her grandmother when *Star Trek: The Original Series* was cancelled, so sci-fi is in the blood too. Alongside a love of love and an adoration for her first love of epic fantasy.

K. B. Thorne is the evolution of Mia Darien after years of learning and living. She has taken both of those things to become a smarter, better writer with a fresh new face and take on the literary world. Thorne writes the urban fantasy, fantasy and sci-fi, while Sadie Johnston writes the romance.

These days, when she's not desperately trying to find time to write, she works as a freelance editor/cover artist/formatter and happily lives her unconventional life alongside her very own Named Man of the North and their mini-tank. (Who is, you know, their son.)

You can find K. B. at authorkbthorne.com!

OTHER BOOKS BY K. B. THORNE

Writing as K. B. Thorne
Blood Rights Series

Bad Blood
Blood and Thunder
Blood Moon
Written in Blood
Bloodshot
First Blood
Out for Blood
New Blood
Flesh and Blood

Out for Blood Series
Bones & Blood

Bellator (Anthology)
Good Things (Anthology)
Ashes to Sunrise (Anthology)
The Shape of Tomorrow (Anthology)
Born of Defiance (Anthology)

Writing as Sadie Johnston (Romance)
Beauty
Help Wanted (with Viola Dawn)
Threnody (with Alastair Malone)
Here, Kitty Kitty (Anthology)
Amor Vincit Omnia (Anthology)
Second Chances (Anthology)